Traveling in the Gait of a Fox

International Authors Series

The Silent Duchess by Dacia Maraini

Chronicle in Stone by Ismael Kadare

Broken April by Ismael Kadare

Dacia Maraini

Traveling in the Gait of a Fox

Poetry 1983-1991

Translated by Genni Gunn

QUARRY PRESS
INTERNATIONAL AUTHORS SERIES

Copyright © Dacia Maraini, 1991
Translation copyright © Genni Gunn, 1992

All rights reserved.

Traveling in the Gait of a Fox was originally published in Italian under the title *Viaggiando con passo di volpe: Poesie 1983-1991* by Rizzoli Libri, Milan.

Canadian Cataloguing in Publication Information

Maraini, Dacia
    Traveling in the gait of a fox: poetry,
1983-1991

(International Authors Series)
Translation of: Viaggiando con passo di volpe.
ISBN 1-55082-055-9

    1. Gunn, Genni, 1949– . II. Title.   III.
Series: International writers series (Kingston, Ont.).

PQ4873.A69B4313 1992 851'.914 C92-090587-0

Cover art by Paul Delvaux, reproduced by permission of Rizzoli Libri.

Design by Keith Abraham.
Typesetting by Susan Hannah.
Printed and bound in Canada by Best-Gagné, Toronto, Ontario.

Published by
Quarry Press, Inc.,
P.O. Box 1061, Kingston, Ontario K7L 4Y5

Contents

8	Introduction by Dacia Maraini
15	traveling in the gait of a fox
16	I am two
17	I bore a poppy
18	war in a plate
20	longing for a journey
21	if your voice enamors me
22	I know you will not come tonight
23	my nights
24	if by loving too much
25	what does it think, the mirror on the wall?
26	the stage flies
27	my days
28	gentlemen gentlemen gentlemen
29	a dark man
30	if only we departed
31	from the belly of gothic arches
32	tomorrow morning at seven
33	a carousel in Tibidabo
35	how many times
36	a young man with eyes of silk
37	I remember a sweet deluge

38	the mountains are short
39	the telephone rings
41	in a shadowy cloister
42	a joyous morning
43	what is a father for
44	sightless eye
45	swinging on a withered branch
46	two spiked shoes
48	I ask my body
49	he was the sweetest son of the moon
50	to swallow all the soup
51	the bat flies low
52	now Julian walks barefoot
54	I wanted to write verses
55	we are so faithless
56	the white of your white
57	leaning tower of the station
58	the last delirium of youth
59	from trip to trip
60	a dead baby
61	I passed the night
62	facetious he was facetious
63	your face has no name
64	to where do you fly my scarf?
65	your lies
66	one foot ahead one foot behind

68	don't push me to cruelty
69	lemon, hot water and a clot of blood
70	the music took him by the chin
71	I dreamt of flying
72	for a father he had a mother
73	in the palm of the right hand
74	a scented evening
75	tranquil thoughts fly
76	millennium of lies
77	tomorrow our muses
78	a small woman with medusa eyes
79	an open window
80	percale hankies
81	the stall door is wide open
82	if you don't come tonight
83	half an hour of denigration
84	if I traveled like a journey
85	does money smell?
86	from far far away
87	I'm alone, you say
88	a flying comet
89	the telephone
90	it will be necessary to emerge from under water
91	something has happened
92	overturned tower: change to come
94	a wicker armchair

Introduction

Why the journey? Why in "the gait of a fox"?

For five years I lived with Marianna Ucrìa in my novel *The Silent Duchess*. Then she was gone. I, who can never reread my books, lost her from sight. And she left in the "Viennese" shoes her daughter, Giuseppa, disparaged as "out of style."

Thus I discovered that those shoes were not mine, nor were those thoughts. The fact is that characters remain true only to themselves. It is we who change, and there is something mysterious and crude in our changing that keeps us on the lookout, never satiated, never content.

Now I try to step into other shoes, into other thoughts, and I do succeed and progress, although I have yet to find a character like Marianna who grabbed me by the sleeve with such impudence, who lodged herself into parts of my heart with such determination.

And yet, superimposed on the silences of the wait, a voice says things that sound secretly familiar. Listening to this voice, I have learned to discern small conclusive geometries, the signs when a thought takes form from small accumulated tingles of life and settles in a drowsy, naked mind.

I am speaking of the intrigues of words we call poems — which convey a serious lightness of birth, an overflowing freedom. Without long-term ties, without devised plans, without structures in full relief.

Not that technique is irrelevant in poetry. On the contrary. Even meter, now in disuse, is necessary. Not to mention the almost carnal knowledge of ancient and modern poets. And certainly to translate is also a good way to understand and to experiment with, mimetically, the complications of the language.

Sometimes, it appears that certain linguistic processes are like the illnesses of plants: tumultuous growths which produce, on trunks, marvelous deformities in the form of dragons, mountains, crevasses.

Is not metaphor in some way an illness of language, an obstruction, a superimposition of lymphs which entwine themselves according to a generous idea of growth?

What else can I say? That these poems were born like this, like small coagulations of thoughts in the empty moments of my full days. And yet they are never there as symbols or substitutions for something else. I have never mixed genres. Except in the case of Marianna, a special character who had the strength to pass from one genre to another, from novel to theatre, without too much damage, with the droll confidence of a deafmute.

Sometimes, while leaned over a work of words, I feel I have the competence of a mason: clean the bricks, lay the lime, draw the line, measure, put one brick on top of the other. Work which takes many years and much patience.

In the Dionysian intensity of playwriting, however, the image that strikes me is the excavation of a well. One descends into the belly of the earth, works in the dark. Something must emerge which resembles a bucket of good drinking water.

Instead, by venturing a foot on the firecracker that is the dance of poetry, I perform precise feats, placing a curtain in front of an open landscape, in the shade of some beautiful pine.

But why the journey? And why in "the gait of a fox?"

The journey is my friend. A friend I have known since childhood. When I was one, I embarked on a ship for Japan. At three, I was traveling between Sapporo and Kyoto. Since then I have always continued, from country to country, from city to city, with the slightly distracted perseverance of one who knows the bitter and unmistakeable taste of nomadism.

But is one nomadic by birth or does one become so? Is nomadism a character trait or a taste acquired through experience? Where does this all-consuming attraction for movement come from?

There are those who think that one travels in order to escape from something, someone, first of all from oneself. There are those who consider it a surrender to the oldest mythologies of alienation.

For others, the journey is instead the primary state of the human being, the sigh of an inquietude that distances us from the wary eyes of the gods. But is Ulysses only a distant cousin, or a brother, or in fact myself?

Certainly, by traveling constantly one risks the loss of the stability of relationships. Every affection tends to be dangerously watered down, to fade. Except for those times when it provokes the opposite effect, rejuvenating stale relationships through distance. But these are meteors destined to extinguish quickly.

The traveler does not possess a real house, and even if he has, in his heart, he has lost it long ago. The tastes of the return are not those of foods eaten daily and recognizable with the eyes closed. The shadows he finds on re-entering don't have the same freshness of those within which he lives daily.

One never knows what to find on a return from a trip. Are we really the same persons as before? Each time a small twinge tells us that we are something other than what we were, and we watch ourselves running, flapping our arms, but unable to fly, as if we were weighed down by two wings filled with sodden feathers.

The traveler must be disposed at any moment, to leave the things he considers most dear, most his, to go and search his own essence in other places, breathe the air of other rooms, sprawl in other beds, cast his eyes through other windows, on other landscapes, other natures.

The traveler may also become confused, prey to winds, lie back in an airplane and think that he has discovered the multiplicity of the universe. He can become dependent on the liquor of movement and drink himself to death. There is nothing to remind him of himself in those senseless wanderings, nothing to recall him to his footprints, to his scents. He cruelly discovers himself as someone else in the morning when he awakens, foreign, in a new bed. Impermanence can render him diffident like a sailor who has lost his compass and sees in the ocean a punishing and evil father.

The moralists say that traveling disperses in extension what should fall into depth. But where is it written that depth is vertical? There is the penetration of things that extend in front of us like the mysterious roads of a milky way.

In fact does not the world itself travel at a dizzy speed? does not the universe itself run, crash, breathe, expand? To where? Till when? Are we not all inside a cosmic breath of alternate rhythms? Will we end projected into nothingness or be trapped inside a heavy block, as large as the fist of a child who will contain within himself the whole universe?

The journey being a metaphor, the most ambiguous and seductive of metaphors it is said, can even be born from immobility. There is no need constantly to subject the body to travel. It's hot, there are flies, illnesses. All it takes to travel on the waves of imagination is to close one's eyes and sit in a chair in the shade. Isn't this what books are for?

But one journey does not exclude another; in fact, it accompanies it greedily. This is at least what happens to me. I don't read anywhere as well as I do in a room that isn't mine, among objects that only belong to me for one night, for a few hours, without the danger of being disturbed by a telephone, a call, a visit, a duty.

Therefore, the pleasure is double: to move the body and free the mind. There is no compensation, no chase. It is the fragrant precariousness of a new color, a strange light, that bestows the attention our minds need in order to settle patiently over letters to decipher.

That there is an erotic waiting in this wandering through cities and countries can't be negated. And it does not last long in the company of a gentle, quiet companion. Rather, in the perspective in which distant and marvelous phantasms of our most disturbing dreams materialize in remote unexpected places, leaving us happily surprised. It's this surprise that enchants us, even if it is slow to appear, and moves us from one journey to another, because we are always waiting for it to materialize.

However, the why of nomadism does not have, for me, true answers. The question stays with me. Now and then, I stop with open book, pen in hand and ask myself: Why am I here and not at home? Why is it that at every invitation, be it a conference, a meeting, a seminar, I feel elated and ready to travel?

Has perhaps not having a family been a premise to the painful freedom of traveling? It's difficult to say. There was a moment when I wanted to shut myself in a house, seal the windows and cuddle a son who would have my pale eyes.

I tried and conceived a child who did have blue eyes. It was confirmed by the doctor who pulled him out, dead, from my body. I don't really know what killed him. An ill-placed placenta or perhaps an irresistible desire for flight, an intolerance to the world, which drove him to leave before he even had shoes on his feet.

Had he been born and grown, I probably would have stopped traveling. I know that he would have had a beautiful smile, slightly ironic, variegated, shadowy, like that of my father who enchanted me when I was a child.

Or perhaps, I would have taken him with me on trips. Certainly. He too would have been possessed by the demon of vagabondage, like my father before me and like his mother before him. My English grandmother, Joy Crosse Pawloska, of whom I keep a black and white photograph on a side-table — the sweetest oval face, eyes slanted at the temples, slightly oriental perhaps because of her Polish blood, the small hands, the robust legs of a walker.

She left her husband and two children to go on a trip by herself, my adventurous grandmother. It was in the first decade of the century. And she wrote novels and travel books. She had a talent for writing, like her grandmother before her, the old Cornelia Berkeley, who had taken pen in hand in order to defend her scientist husband, Andrew Crosse (1784-1855), who was accused of what heresy I don't know.

My grandmother, Joy, it appears, did the opposite of what women often do: stay at home to grasp children by the ankles while the husbands leave, travel, dream, flirt, love, remarry, earn, learn.

It is futile to wonder whether she was driven by egoism or sublime courage. Cowardice or enraptured love. Certainly she didn't travel just to travel, but to pursue one of her lovers, not the one she wed later, in a second marriage. Later landing in Rome, meeting my grandfather, Antonio, and deciding to settle in Florence unconcerned about the scandal.

And that, I think, is the origin of the subterranean tension which has marked my few years in Florence. A vague taste of "immorality" that still perfumed the air of Torre di Sopra, the villa del Poggio, when I arrived from Japan, before departing for Palermo, my mother's homeland.

In spite of the gravel paths, in spite of the neoclassical statues, in spite of the calm composures, I knew at the bottom of my heart that ours was a "different" family.

On the other hand, hadn't my father and mother broken with fascism, broken with their parents, broken with their friends, in order to go wandering in the distant island of Hokkaido, after only a year of marriage?

I know for sure that by traveling, I distance myself from myself, so much so as to lose sight of myself. And this gives me peace. But at the same time, it unsettles me. So much so, that I have a sudden need to grab myself by the hair, to slap myself, to nail my hands to the typewriter, to stay, this time, stay and face those things due to me, with competence and determination.

But as soon as I finger the beads, counting off days, they suddenly appear identical and interchangeable. Time flakes through my fingers and strips off my skin. I know that, by staying, I will end up with no skin at all, with a susceptibility to the breaths of air that will freeze me.

Traveling, Melville writes, "is a way of driving off the spleen and regulating the circulation. Whenever I find myself growing grim about the mouth; whenever it is a damp, drizzly November in my soul; whenever I find myself involuntarily pausing before coffin warehouses, and bringing up the rear of every funeral I meet; and especially whenever my hypos gets such an upper hand of me that it requires a strong moral principle to prevent me from deliberately stepping into the street, and methodically knocking people's hats off — then, I count it high time to get to sea as soon as I can . . . ."

An impatience, in short, primarily physical, the urgency of what is alive in our body, blood and lymphs which claim the necessary distancing from the cruelty of being ourselves, here, now.

And so I resume to plan departures. And they will contain, in their itineraries, the certainty of return. And those returns will be joyous and cherished; they will give me, I know, a great desire for stillness. Because this is the game of coming and going, that somehow resembles the chain of days with its dawns and sunsets.

Regarding "the gait of a fox," for me it's a matter of a rhythm, a course, a style. Nothing that recalls the shrewdness and the ferocity that often distinguish foxes. What I like about this sister of the wolf is her silent lightness, her nocturnal curiosity, her love for shadows and for woods.

When I was a child in Sapporo, a small indomitable woman whom I called Okachan would tell me stories about gentle, trembling, white foxes that would come out on moonlit nights to sit at the edge of wells. In the Japanese fables, the fox is none other than a woman who has undergone an enchantment, who has been transformed into an animal because of forbidden love or forbidden pregnancy.

Therefore, by "the gait of a fox" I mean this nocturnal roaming in the glimmer of the moon, among shadows of unknown woods, with weightless paws, a nose that follows scents in the search of wild berries and small watermelons to bring to the den. No one would think of shooting a fox that is resting on the edge of a well. Within her fur might be hidden a small female figure who is in love with mystery.

Dacia Maraini

traveling in the gait of a fox

traveling in the gait of a fox
how bitter the airs
on a morning of departure
how senseless the steps
between one station and another
between one breath and another
while we
I, vagabond
and you, sedentary quietist
continue a flight
the taste of bananas and black clouds
we call each other long distance
how are you? and you?
I'm afraid of this future
I swallow
while touring the world
with shameless steps
I'd like you with me
but you're not there
you who always stay home
you who understand absence
I pack my bags
depart
you remain
and tomorrow morning goodbye
but where I'm going
there are no more airplanes
there are no more trains
there are no more stations
there is not even a journey
are you well? and you?
tomorrow morning I'll leave
with or without my bags
because what awaits me below
is the nostalgia of return

I am two

I am two people
it's obvious now
I am two plus one
minus one and this makes two
twice I was born
and twice have died
twice have been lost
and perhaps once more
because two and one are three
the times I've thrashed myself
and once I even retched
but maybe they were two
given that four of me
pull me by the feet
while I sleep, in dragon voice
and only once I've loved
but at least two hundred times
touched happiness
but I have not been born two hundred times
because at onehundredandninetynine
I became bored and thus
between one and two, forgot myself
and if I were not two, I would be zero
but one is me and the other is two
therefore take me as I am
two of one and one of two

I bore a poppy

I bore a poppy
from my beautiful red skirts
my love they say
is a soldier without a war
when the poppy will bear me
I will be born anew like a damsel
with long green eyelashes
and the yearn for a poppy on the chin

war in a plate

war in a plate
but only for curious eyes:
a woman pulls a dead girl
by the arm
a house breaks to pieces
biscuit walls crumble
how many times have we talked of war
seated, peacefully
at either side of the table?
in the air, a car tumbles
on the salad bowl
a man screams staring at the void
in his bloody pant leg
a war overseas
surges on the gigantic screen
explodes, unravels, lacerates
our profane thoughts,
what will we call
the ghosts of others' suffering, my god
if not descendants, secretions
of an elated heart?
a war beyond the bread
consumes itself during dinner
fields burn
a school burns
a forest burns
the terraces of a luxury hotel burn
while we filet the fish
a boy laughs triumphantly
he has lost all his teeth,
a war overseas
and we who pry, wary
beyond a pearly glass
drink beer
inside a violet evening
and listen, surprised
to the sound of a motor,

is the war outside or inside?
will the plane explode
or slide through clouds?
a girl runs, barefoot
a child cries soundless
we are not watching the war
it is spying on us
beyond the double striped screen
another grenade
a helmet flies
the body of a soldier
soft and inert folds into itself
a war overseas
falls sweetly into our plate
and we eat it with the potatoes
or does it eat us
like many shovelled sons
ruining forever
the carnal experience of sorrow?

longing for a journey

longing for a journey
my child
would you come to Peru
with me, without suitcases
blue running shoes
on your feet?

if your voice enamors me

if your voice enamors me
where will I put my feet
between piazza Flaminio and the Tiber
where will I lay myself
if your whirling
dripping, relentless voice
widens my ear
like the voice of the dead
who walk fresh
on via dei Gracchi on holiday?
we are near and
don't know each other
two birds that fly
different skies
without suitcases
without licences
without even a kind idea of ourselves
yet I feel
I know you well
your voice is sumptuous
soft and laughing
with a hidden thorn of cruelty
you entered my house
like a thief of words
through a receiver, polite
and now we say goodbye
like two poor friends
without an if or a but,
sensible as two lawyers
suspended in time
like a drowsy breath

I know you will not come tonight

I know you will not come tonight
and tomorrow you'll be sorry
for not coming
and for being sorry

my nights

my nights
of bitter orange
were inhabited
by awkward white whales
and flying serpents,
I recognized the swing
of milk-white curtains,
I planted a medlar tree
in the bowl of a dead dog
out sprung a sapling
twisted and angry
which I will call extinction
my nights
of sweet jasmine
how strong were the wings
and liquid the memories
in that distant untamed island
where every morning
I awakened taller
and happier
my nights
of valerian
have become dark and shameless
and however much I lay
my head on feathered pillows
in upturned cities
inside strange rooms
I no longer dream of whales
my nights
of diazepam
tighten my shoulders
how will I summon the swallow
that carries my life in its beak?

if by loving too much

if by loving too much
we end up not loving at all
I say that
love is a bitter ruse
those eyes, half-mast
sail and sail
on waves of milk
my god, what hides
behind those blue eyelids
a thought of flight
a scheme of defiance
a decision to possess?
the ship with black sails
now turns westward
glides on waves of foam
among swirls of snow
and famished gulls
I know that on that bridge
I'll leave a shoe, a tooth
and a good part of me

what does it think, the mirror on the wall?

what does it think, the mirror on the wall?
what does it think, the book in the shelf?
what does it think, the plate in the buffet?
what does it think, my dress hung in the sun?
perhaps the mirror dreams
the book will talk and the book dreams
the plate will dance and the plate
dreams my dress hung in the sun
will tell a story of small seductions

the stage flies

the stage flies
and we cling to her sails
in our ears mute music
the sound of untuned drums
and we dance like trained fleas
eat salami sandwiches
sit with feet in the air
is it you who laughs or someone behind you?
never as in this passage from yesterday to tomorrow
have we been overcome by anguish and wounds
our mouths full of mushrooms
which spring among the chairs of the audience,
the desire to risk, my god, what is it?
the face of the bureaucrat laughs eternally
and I who wanted to sing the fury
of an Antigone who buries her brothers
under the planks of the stage
between January and March
in a year of crimes and losses
we are there to part a red curtain,
the bloody curtain of a bloodless theater
while everyone laughs convinced it is day
under a spotlight of orange gel
without thinking of the dead
who wander, frantic,
in jeans and t-shirts
asking to be buried
joyfully, while from above
a stagehand spits sunflower seeds

my days

my days
the color of hydrangeas
under shadowy porches
and flaxen terraces,
I have long inhabited
in desolation
now I feel as if I'm eating
ripened grapes stolen from wasps
I return to search those shadows
and find only brilliant photographs

gentlemen gentlemen gentlemen

gentlemen gentlemen gentlemen
with lingering glances
with sucked-in bellies
with quick shoes
over steep streets
not too long ago
a woman lost herself,
gentlemen who drink wine
who lower dusky eyes over cheeks
have you by chance seen a shabby woman
with dull cobalt eyes
lost in some station
with a suitcase full of books
a tongue sealed in her mouth
like a worthless possession?

a dark man

a dark man
tells me yes then tells me no
he wears a beret on his ears
has the gait of a ballerina
eyes and hands milk-white
he is sincere as a sparrow
gentle as a bee in flight
he cuts my heart with a knife
then, merciful, wants to heal it
my love makes him uneasy
yet he feasts on it
as if from an old-fashioned delicacy

if only we departed

if only we departed
from here towards evening
if only we departed
we would not be appeased
and would leave, unmoored, but we would leave
and this is the theory of postponed journeys
if only departures had the breath of thieves
we would leave towards evening
with our tongues sealed in our mouths
the journey has a middle-car
which does not stop at stations in use
the journey being a stop
we are experts at split voyages
more than anything at departures and returns
perhaps we would not return if our house were not
another journey glimpsed from the window
and between the coming and going
there is the staying which is a way of beginning anew
from where we have not departed
we are gone but won't come back
because the return occurred years ago
and the journey now is a weight on our feet
if we hadn't already departed
now I could leave content
because I know I would return,
for we, travelers by birth
smell the unmistakeable scent
of a return begun and never completed

from the belly of gothic arches

from the belly of gothic arches
at night
a greedy child looks out
to watch the bungling
of a saturnine mother
and he dances on one foot
dances like a top
this child born so many years ago

tomorrow morning at seven

tomorrow morning at seven
we'll pack our bags
meanwhile the night sleeps
and the curtains fly
and the lime-tree breathes
and the mint appropriates
the manger of wolves
and the roses open slowly
and the doves perch on the window-sills
and you don't call
and everything takes a turn for the worse
I slip a finger in my mouth
take a false step
fall in order to get up
get up in order to fall,
what demon tricks the senses
what blows air
on my neck like the cold breath
of a gentle vampire?

a carousel in Tibidabo

a carousel in Tibidabo
and Barcellona
faded and green
the scent of pine in the nostrils
an avalanche of children
a Gaudi shell
to collect our breaths
you carried your violin
stuck to your fingers
like in the Dali painting
do you remember the heat
of Barcellona in August?
from your trousers sprung
timid, small curious pigeons,
the Sagrada Famiglia
bodies killed in the pretence
of eternal harmony
Jesus, Joseph and Mary
the encounter on the stairs
in the lace of emptiness
a hundred tendernesses for a massacre
one afternoon do you remember
you dragged me to the bullfight
a bull roared, covered in faeces
flanks glossy
with blood and sweat
and that blond dancer who
the public, obscene, applauded
and there was a man with an amputated leg
do you recall? and the ice-cream vendor
the me who always falls into the other
made herself bull
and with him died in the crowd
and later later later
between the olive leftovers
I drank cold tea

my kerchief on the lamp
a chinese brothel you called it
we kissed like fish
the bull in our eyes
someone put the suitcases
behind the door
the mosquitoes camped
on our naked arms
the recollection of a Spanish August
makes the milk curdle in my veins

how many times

how many times
in crowded streets
among overheated cars
and the smell of stray cats
have we entwined our eyes
like bouquets of daisies
while our feet dance
to the rhythm of breaths

a young man with eyes of silk

a young man with eyes of silk
the spitting image of his father
he and I on the bed of change
he liked black stockings
garters taut as whips
on the white skin of thighs
short slips
and stiletto heels
he was a gentle young man
with a nostalgia for death
under the covers he would cross himself
then laugh, exhausted
a young man with eyes of black silk

I remember a sweet deluge

I remember a sweet deluge
a light falling of stones
perhaps the chattering bird
perched on the branch under my window
yesterday morning,
with nun's shoes on my feet
I will climb those blustery paths
so many hanging clothes
so many limp collars
under a lamp a man reads
seated, hands in his lap,
the neon sign of the smoke shop
casts a square light,
the cautious gait of a cat
leaves wet triangles on the asphalt
I wait for the return of a man
I loved a million years ago

the mountains are short

the mountains are short
and to climb them hurts the heart
the line on the horizon so brief
but we needed only a glance
of accord, so many lies in that theater
the color of the sea, inside which wandered
the fish of thoughts
gasping for breath in their essential need to die
on a dry shore
too dry and the actor was the actor
his untouchable body clad
in the perfidy of words, and above were spot lights
and costumes of wonders,
tell me when will we begin again
thrice over, with joy and desperation
one shoe inside the other like Chinese women
the need for a stage stirs our senses
and we will cry together seated in the dark
thinking of what we could have been
and are not

the telephone rings

the telephone rings
an extended voice
and he, the other, the loved one
does not answer, does not speak
imagination can walk
limping a little
like an old soldier
a survivor of distant wars
who now wants to sleep
but also stroll
and the walking both drains him
and lures him
in a faint immoderate voice
twisted, vulgar
the soldier needs
his own solitary war
his own trenches dug
carefully in nocturnal thoughts,
he delights and grieves
at the voice which the telephone
denies him, smiling stern
the telephone rings and rings
beyond the city, the piazzas
beyond sweet salty waters
the telephone rings and no one replies
in the parched cavity of thought
night falls from above
with the precision
of a warplane
between drowsy eyelashes
and veiled eyes

if the voice has vanished
in the wires, the soldier waits
gloriously weightless
for that voice
to arrive by telephone
like a ferocious tempest
to disturb the perfumed tranquil airs
of that unkempt garden
called the heart

in a shadowy cloister

in a shadowy cloister
an albino nun
was reading a book
wings flattened against her head
small blazing eyes
long curly lashes
beautiful waxen hands,
what is the albino nun reading
in the shadowy cloister
of early morning
the abbess asked herself
suddenly aware that she loved her
with a pious, rash love

a joyous morning

a joyous morning
my mouth full of nails
I awaken and don't know
if I should get up
a sparrow has tumbled
into the teeth of the cat
who gently carries it to me
without crushing it
a gift
but where did you get it?
the cat sniggers
flaunting its prey,
I have stone hands
I have stone feet
but where, where will I find
the proof of wrongdoing?
I'll have to get up
free my hands
put my feet on the ground
I'll have to save
the bird from the hunter
but I plunge into sleep
and in my neck
feel the pressure of teeth
of one who parades me
with inordinate joy
in a flutter of thoughts
while one by one
hours become days
and days become years

what is a father for

what is a father for
if later his son
becomes his mother
in hushed afternoons
in stuffed chairs
inside arid laps
and pork cutlets
that son
was born flawed
an eye hung on his neck
a belly full of needs
his father wanted to devour him
his mother wrapped a stone
and shot it in his father's mouth
who swallowed it
assuming it was
the cursed child,
what is a father for
if later his son
makes fun of him
and of his ancient religious appetite?

sightless eye

sightless eye
silent sorrow
but if the eye, flying,
knows how to glide
between the folds of a tender thought
if the eye is a horse
that gallops beyond the oceans
if the eye sees because it can create
and it creates with knowledge
unknown but surmised
is it still knowledge or pure will
the barbed thought
that envelops the horse
and makes him fly back
to a time without sorrow
when the small eggs of march
are suspended in an eternal return?

swinging on a withered branch

swinging on a withered branch
we kissed breathless
the branch creaked
but did not snap
when the owl sang
we broke apart
to stare at the night
which ambled
like a crippled frog
but in that moment the branch
broke
and we fell
and are falling still

two spiked shoes

two track shoes
two light feet
a field of wheat
and new shoots
in my laughing dream
where angels were birds
and the wheat glittered green
greener than the sky,
in that dream I was falling in love
with a football player with sabre eyes
breathless, I followed him
in a field of violet borders
where wheat grew tall
and the body of the young man leaped
between new shoots
behind an invisible ball
among invisible players
with the ferocity
of a victory to gain
the white and black body of the young man,
in a field bristly with lilac borders
made me suddenly fall in love
I began to lose my sight in that green veiled lake
a young body in flight
two light feet
a breath of bitter almond
that football player
was the focus of my languid eye
and that body ran
and I slept
and he played
and I watched
a trumpet of voices
awakened me
crying "goal!"

and the green wavering field
and the solitary football player
with his white and black body
his invisible ball
his light shoes
all vanished
in the familiar warmth of the pillow

I ask my body

I ask my body
my waiting body
what is that sorrow doing
perched between ribs
idle, chattering bird
what are you doing there, alone
stunned, senseless, stripped
I ask my body,
my waiting body
what are those pangs
beneath the curves of my breasts
meek solitary bees
that suck milk
from the wreaths of the senses,
could it be, I ask myself
that the bees will eat my heart
that the bird will eat the bees
and that sorrow will nest
in the void of my breast?

he was the sweetest son of the moon

he was the sweetest son of the moon
and truly loved two women
one who inhabited his thoughts
and one who walked in her shoes
from one side of the ocean to the other
he planted nails of silk
familiar with charm
but not pity, the beautiful young man
for courage, he had only teeth
that nipped like goats
the sweetest son of the moon

to swallow all the soup

to swallow all the soup
is not for me
yet I eat and run
and laugh and tell everyone I'll manage
you won't go far
a breathless wise man tells me
and I drink mint tea
and grope toward death

the bat flies low

the bat flies low
perches breathless
on a dry well
the plane-tree whips
its sick leaves
covers itself in resin drops
we pull the cords
of a grass theatre
in this fine summer
with frayed edges
a summer theatre
in the belly of villa Borghese
among paper marches and other prodigal citizens
a tenacious Roman dream
the theatre of vegetables
with its brown and blue curtains
its earthen floor
trailed by yellow roots
like hardened elbows
our thoughts fly
toward the light of a confused logic
ready to become flesh and word
under the enraptured game of the spotlights,
villa Borghese is languid
toward seven in the evening
in a milk of sleeping leaves
we hear the roar of a lion
behind the wall of the zoo
in the giant aviary
an imprisoned eagle flies furiously
we pull on the curtain
with its bordered edges
to cover the stage
from our excessive artifices
a ladybird perches on a finger
light, enameled, red and black
she resembles the back
of a teaspoon from Sevres,
I swear she'll bring us luck

now Julian walks barefoot

now Julian walks barefoot
now Julian eats frozen roses
now Julian all the cats have escaped
from your lap, not even a flea
takes you for its father
in a room in Cinecittà
you ate pasta and beans
from a plastic plate
Julian, hands soiled with green lacquer
you spoke of freedom
mouth full, eyes laughing
nearly white, so filled
with air they were
Julian, what was the theatre
under your arid feet,
split into warm and bitter zones
between bursts of imagined reality
the geometry of your intelligence
the colorless language of the ascetic
made you a fierce monk
but you liked to touch walls
and bodies and machines and earth
Julian with the face of a predatory bird
you smoked like an old Turk
slid inside black pants
along the trails of thought
and Judith who puffed her hair
into the wing of a wild owl
seeking gold, you and she, hunched
under the planks of the stage
digging furiously, this is how she was born
like a mouse between flying spotlights

and you followed with the grace
of an acrobat in brilliant
winter evenings between glass panels
and Dutch curtains, among taffeta flowers
and paper crowns, Julian when you look at us
we will already be far
and you, the great archer, from your world
of shrill silences will observe us
through inverted binoculars
and we will salute each other as if from a distant ship
waving a hand and a white rag

I wanted to write verses

I wanted to write verses
but had no paper
in the bathtub
a black fur
rose from gray bubbles
I searched with fingers
in my soft, drenched pocket
found a notebook
but it was half-melted
and so I began
to write with my lipstick
on a clean plate
but what I wrote
I'll never know
I awakened
with my hands soiled in red

we are so faithless

we are so faithless
one to the other
we blow air between fingers
and say we love each other
he was a child prodigy
his eighty years hung around his ears
like coral cherries
he stood on one foot only
his mother shot a nail into his heart
and he suddenly lost his vampire teeth
the thrush died
the wasps died
inside the dark house no one remained
his mother sits on the balcony
I stretch on his pillow
and he doesn't know whether to win like a gentleman
or submit to an irreparable loss
sweet, calm, sibylline

the white of your white

the white of your white
painted eyes
you wear running shoes
walk like a soldier
eat bitter chocolate
what are those
small wounds on your hand
I saw mice
who thought they were pigs
you swell and swell
a duck sang like a swan
the final song
from the shoals of delusions
don't eat bread any more
I beg you, said that woman
called Undine
and she fell in love with a fresh-water prince

leaning tower of the station

leaning tower of the station
neon pink and violet
a boy sweeps the rails
another watches the street
the tobacconist leans from the counter
we will bring cream sweets
into that house only women inhabit
there will be dogs barking
small birds and dead babies
walking among zinnias
the arbour covers the shutters
you arrive running
it's already night, already winter
we kiss like lovers in the movies
mouths against mouths saying I love you
the train departs strident
and you are not here
I saw you laugh for a moment
and then die like the flare of a match

the last delirium of youth

the last delirium of youth
vanished subtleties, broken eyes
how fresh is the new-born morning!
my life, how you wither
unaware and lose one by one
the most stupid and sensual desires
my life, how you flee
without looking back
no wind in your mouth
among horizons of houses
in a bustle of enemy shoes
if only you'd stop
you'd know all has already occurred
between the wine and the fruit
on that flowered tablecloth
in a day of delights
yet it would be right and clean
to die without decline
to close the mouth without farewells
to put on cardboard shoes
and tread on sand hills
in the joy of an impossible return
but pain dies slowly
and loses itself in the paths of the eyes
a new curiosity
springs between thoughts of death
heavy eyelids
open to the day
which emerges from its egg
and the joy of life
creeps under the tongue

from trip to trip

from trip to trip
he discovered
he had crossed rivers and forests
but of the woman
who slept in his bed
who had the name of a flower
he had no inkling . . .

a dead baby

a dead baby
in my womb, was it yesterday
or tomorrow? a dead baby
with long blond eyelashes
and pink fingers
a baby departed
feet wrapped in cotton-wool
canine teeth protruding
a baby with no wish to speak
perhaps he will be buried
in soil replete
with maternal love
husk and walnut
life and shroud
within a nocturnal pod
the baby has refused forever
to say yes
and now laughs at me
from the depths of a foreign night

I passed the night

I passed the night
tossing on crumpled sheets
in a tangle of dreams
a single cherry on a plate
while the wind rose,
in your future
I am a fresh-water stone
waiting to receive
your good-luck kiss,
perhaps tomorrow
we will span dirty waters
in a walnut shell,
don't call me mother
there are too many arrows
in the bow you embrace
you'll play cards
in front of the marina
in the oiled lamp of night
so much wasted jealousy
there was already a wind
or perhaps it had subsided
I passed the night
waiting to sleep
with you, inside a water dream

facetious he was facetious

facetious he was facetious
hooded eyes
trimmed nails
a curious mixture of intelligence
cowardice and courtesy
and there we were, he and I
we drank together
the blessed water of recognition
he fell in love with me
and I with the father in him
holding hands
like siamese twins
in days of opaque radiance
we loved each other so much
with such harmony and sorrow
that we consumed our love

your face has no name

your face has no name
your voice has no sound
your train has no number
your journey has no hours
but I know you will come
with that face
with that voice
with that train
at the end of your long voyage

to where do you fly my scarf?

to where do you fly my scarf
minus wings minus head
the seabirds have
other frailties, other scents
to where do you fly my scarf
without feathers you cannot depart

your lies

your lies
my love
taste of milk and roses
I drink them without asking why
your lies
my love
make me nauseous
but you do it in kindness
to cause me no sorrow
a lump of feathers in my throat
a walk backwards
how insistent he is, why?
I yearn for a ferrous sincerity
that offends the sight and the senses
you rinse in fresh water,
your lies ring twice
in the voice's echo
in the heartbeat and counterbeat
dance of the senses
but you do it in kindness
I know my love
and, in kindness, you crush
with spiked shoes
those September truths
with no shadows or edges
for you my love
the truth is too cruel
impure and intrusive
and so you renounce it,
stubborn, polite, serene, happy
for love of love, I know
and so my sweetest friend
your sublime lies
which should warm my hands
nail my tongue to the palate
bury my living intelligence
underground

one foot ahead one foot behind

one foot ahead one foot behind
one foot bent one foot aligned
over the threshold, I know
she is getting married, she watches
wary and mute
and her feet follow,
am I entering or leaving?
a calm grips me by the throat
the threshold sees me
cross with my thoughts,
I push a heavy iron gate
I push a light glass door
shadows engulf me,
I span two wings of artificial blooms
grateful for the sway of the boat
that will cross the sacred river,
today I waver one foot to the other,
I know the threshold is watching me
run in the dusky shade
among cold plastic flowers
one foot ahead one foot behind
one foot bent one foot aligned
to cross the threshold
is to arise from one's own ashes
you are your own daughter the arab told me
in his faint, impudent voice
you are the daughter of the mouse
that tunnels your thoughts,
the revelry, my life is over
my feet know that the thrust
across the threshold
is a question of conscience
the girl is there to control the passage
eyes stare at the street
the nose of a woman emerges between dusky windows

I know what escapes me
is not the shadow that swells
not the river of tar
not the marble bread
I eat at the theatre
not the photos in the window
not the voice of the arab
but the sweet sensation of rebirth
that the threshold suggests
there where my feet touch
happily mute on the white and black
oblique tiles
of an invisible and bizarre chessboard

don't push me to cruelty

don't push me to cruelty
I enjoy playing too much
you have the skin of a leopard seal
eyes languid and ferrous
and a liquid intelligence
that makes thoughts bloom
if we eat watermelon
we will have mouths soiled in red
we'll dance in high heels
on a tile floor
don't push me to cruelty
I love cuts and torture
glass in the belly
I will break your heart and then
eat it with basil
I will cover your throat with honey
then bite you
five fingers of joy in your eyes
come, let's dance, make the black of my eyes
drip onto my cheeks
my wise, brave medusa

lemon, hot water and a clot of blood

lemon, hot water and a clot of blood
inside the white cups
ringed in yellow and blue
where at the bottom appeared
a dancing woman
and perhaps also a golden almond-tree,
lemon, hot water and a clot of blood
you climb from sticky depths,
filled with sweet, tepid essences
you taste of mint
"we who are friends," you say,
but what is friendship
I said, you said, we said to each other,
in a world of trifles
how shabby and faded
seems that stolen hidden thing
called affection

the music took him by the chin

the music took him by the chin
young deer without sorrows
filled his throat with perfumes
gave him the hands of a fairy
the gestures of a magician
and a bottle of cavalier wisdom
for bravery
the music his empress
put feathers on his feet
and sent him through the world
with so much love
it left him blind and triumphant

I dreamt of flying

I dreamt of flying
so many times at once
once many times,
weightless above roofs
breathing black joy
perched on cornices
balanced on roof-ridges
how often
I've walked the etherial highways
of the horizon
among salty clouds and rays of sun
the only companions
of a drowsy conscience
a gull with pointed beak
and a sparrow with bitter wings
I'd like to know how to fly
again in dreams, fly again
like a swallow
from one roof tile to another
and spit on the heads
of passersby and laugh
at their surprise, is it raining?
or are those tears of a sick god?
I still fly, but in the respites of dreams
my foot, heavy
now stumbles, my hand clutches
an eave which detaches
flying I want to fly
and refill with joy
the thorns of darkness

for a father he had a mother

for a father he had a mother
hung around his neck
like an old cloak
a lick of the paws
at the waking hour
my soldier who sings Bach
and kicks history
you are the son of an irascible womb
you have suckled at dry
ink-black nipples, poor king
what will you do with yourself?

in the palm of the right hand

in the palm of the right hand
I hold a headless man
and his blue car,
in the palm of the left
I hold a well
with sprigs of elder and yellow canes.
if I close my hands in prayer
I will put the headless man
and his blue car
into the well
with tall elders
and yellow canes

a scented evening

a scented evening
and the lights are out
the air, calm, vibrant
come, come my vampire
we will be home alone
I will bare my neck
close my eyes to the bite
hold back the scream when
teeth puncture
tender, naked flesh
come, come my vampire
it's almost midnight
the windows are open
there is no garlic hung
no crucifixes on walls
no hearts in love with Jesus
to guard the senses
only you and I, I and you
we will look at each other
smile in accord, courteous
in those stagnant airs
docile, I will offer my throat
to your beloved teeth
come, come my vampire
the night is mild and fragrant

tranquil thoughts fly

tranquil thoughts fly
from your blue hands
where will we go tomorrow
between ruins of houses
yours and mine
on that tall beanstalk
grown from seed to tree
that now spreads its branches
on the muffled fields of thought?

millennium of lies

millennium of lies
and stagnant waters
how your eyes drip
laughing delights
pain melts
on my naked hands
with the grace
of lemon ice-cream and
the mills of god grind slowly
why do you wait until a somber Sunday
among broken tiles
and sick donkeys
among horseflies and
flying violins
to tell me you are not alone
and that seduction is an old teacher
from whom you've stolen skills
and now you teach crickets
morning love
with a blessed song that
splits your tongue
into two triumphs of lies

tomorrow our muses

tomorrow our muses
sated and frail
will fall with bored smiles
from their chairs
how cruel the kangaroo
that hides written words in its pouch
thoughts lost
like confetti at feasts
without a wedding
we are the flags of tomorrow, they say
lavish false smiles,
morning and night I don
a jacket with mended sleeves
my shoes walk alone
ice now inhabits my heart
how to play with new words?

a small woman with medusa eyes

a small woman with medusa eyes
two mercurial fins at her ankles
a red bow in her hair
worn short, like a boy
she has been sister, then mother
her milk bitter
we walked and walked in love
under lime-trees
in a whirl of flying seeds
what are you doing now among so many madonnas
painted onto official paintings
joyous onto carnal joys?
time flies, sand flea
midnight has come,
and your slipper is still in the hand of the prince

an open window

an open window
a bared neck
night dangles
with black sails
above the attic
a glass half-moon
cuts the horizon in half
I put down my book
extinguish the lamp
and await a wolf
with the large eyes of a lamb

percale hankies

percale hankies
downfall of planets
the earth dies
within an empty glass

the stall door is wide open

the stall door is wide open
the cow with the star eyes
and the donkey with black curls
remain riveted
to the empty manger
where mice run, content

if you don't come tonight

if you don't come tonight
I know it's revenge
your memory is long
as a serpent
and your tongue sweet
as sherbet

half an hour of denigration

half an hour of denigration
eating grapes
she slipped on gold strands
that were chains

if I traveled like a journey

if I traveled like a journey
I would never be still
eyes on my back
mouth on my nape
how many pairs of shoes have you worn out
gypsy with the peeling nose?

does money smell?

does money smell?
oh the scent of mimosa
oh the scent of fresh coffee
oh the scent of my lover's mouth!
what will I buy tomorrow
with money that smells of mimosa
fresh coffee and my lover's mouth?

from far far away

from far far away
an ant emerged
from the blue receiver
to greet him dancing
on the other side of the sea
she tried to summon her love
but failed, poor thing!

I'm alone, you say

I'm alone, you say
it's amazing
you're amazed too
it's curious, you say
that after having loved so much
and traveled, and read, and joked
after having danced and
chatted and made children
and divorced and remarried three times
and made more children
I'm amazed, you say
that I'm alone, after so much done
and undone, and walking and eating
in the morning when I wake up
you say, I'm still there
old, skeleton full of desires
with all my dead friends behind me
but what am I doing, you say
amazed by your amazement
a graceful light
in your dark sincere eyes

a flying comet

a flying comet
in the window frame
entered from the left
departed from the right
on the wall
a scorched curtain
remains

the telephone

the telephone
black like you
mute like you
laughs at me
behind my back
peals of laughter
while I wash dishes
it's ready to trumpet
every voice
but yours
it keeps secret
like a sphinx
with black whims, of glass

it will be necessary to emerge from under water

it will be necessary to emerge from under water
to wet oneself to the bone
to re-knot those threads of silk
that lead nowhere
it will be necessary to face the night
with its plush lined gloves
and ask the feet
to go where they don't want to go
to greet
the proper baseness

something has happened

something has happened
what I don't know
but your sphinx smile
tells me I can guess
meanwhile your mouth
gently invents
delicate and captious
showcase truths
something has happened
I shouldn't know
in order to keep in balance
your castle of cards

overturned tower: change to come

overturned tower: change to come
she tells me, insistent, the light splits
her face in two triangles, soft blue
you won't have children, she stares at me, sly
see these dead brilliant stars
while he sweats and eats
bitter chocolate at home on the terrace
but I see someone watching
she says and laughs, perplexed in the triangle
crushing her butt in the plate
see here, a dead king, a baby perhaps
and you forgotten, she says and burps
your luck is waning
flowers will grow from nettles,
she laughs, happy, she has kind eyes
the mole on her thumb is an open hole
the knight walks and walks and
the hanging man swings under the moon
there's a black queen with soiled nails
and hair, three suns against the sky
a sign of sexual excesses
someone will trick you, be careful
she's young, the witch, maybe thirty
beautiful, fervent, menacing, intelligent
you'll encounter the queen, she says
don't steer her away, grasp her in hand
while death mows down nettles
and drags buckets of sludge
let's begin with the past
that's already the future, her small
butterfly hands discard, shuffle,
a wolf will abide in your bed, mute
almond eyes and the mouth of a fish
receive him with warmth, love will enrichen
his lips, long roads will yield thorns
and camellias, on those roads
is a lake, that I really don't know

you can cross, but beware
your feet will be drenched, she smiles milky teeth
dead stars fly
through deserts and marshes
two snakes make a knot,
beware of a plight with the law
someone will betray you
rest your head, you vagabond
look, the baby is surfacing, she says,
without arms without legs
meanwhile she shuffles the cards, patient,
if you do haul the bucket
it will be with great effort,
she says, you will kiss, you and he,
but you won't die
the bluish triangle grazes my forehead
the dead stars fly
and the hanged man swings in the evening wind
walk and walk and walk
in the end, you will cross the lake
but will drench your feet, the overturned tower
is good luck, she says and sneezes
the death you carry in your chest will help you live

a wicker armchair

a wicker armchair
sea ruffled in front
you were there calm and absorbed
your eyes soft in time
that unravels, departs, flies
and you with your brisk tenderness
do you remember mint ice-creams?
I was waiting for you, you would say
in the morning at seven
seated in the wicker armchair
in the calm of the threshold
in the shade of the house
in the silence of sleep
already quarrelling with the future
you spun the thread of the wait
between hands, old baobab
while the skies ran
over your tortoise neck
that future gives nothing
that carefree future
with its gentleman airs
and its paper feet
has taken you away
as if it were nothing
betraying my and your trust
and your good humor
your slapdash impatiences
your victor instincts,
you left a cane
I see it every time
I enter and leave the house
its bone head
and glossy redwood body
remind me of yours
limping joyously
among baggage and pillows
while your eyebrows laugh

and your chin disappears
and your feet beat
on the drum of delights
in the blue light
of August in Sabaudia
what will I do without your eyes?
what will I do without your voice?
on that wicker armchair
dear son who
have been my father
in your astral distances
remember the talks in the kitchen
the mornings at seven
while we waited for the water to boil?
and that laughing at ourselves
and those daydreams of mountains
of paper and vapor
with those hands and those feet
that baobab and that drum
I will wait to hear you return